WHILE
I'M STILL
MYSELF

WHILE I'M STILL MYSELF

a collection of short stories

JEREMY MARK LANE

To my wife, who encourages me,
and to my children, who inspire me.

That Winter

It's interesting the way the weather can affect one's mood. The winter, in particular, has been known to give the hardiest of men a case of the blues. It starts with the trees—gray, naked, encircled by the crunchy yellow remnants of spring's beautiful green grass—standing sadly below a dreary, gray sky, and in Texas, where the sun seems to burn hotter and brighter than any place in the world, the chill follows fast and hard. Every year since he was a young child, the first cold snap of winter had created in Gabriel Alexander a foreboding that increased each day until the sun reappeared in late February. There was one winter, however, that of his twenty-second year, that did not have such an impact. That year he barely noticed the cold at all.

He had stumbled upon a small diner in downtown Bluff Dale. "Downtown" being a loosely used term, of course, as he noticed quickly that Bluff Dale barely had enough town to be down in. There was only a road, nicely paved, from which several unpaved roads snaked to the north and south, a deer-processing plant that still stood only by the grace of God, and a small, white house, completely gutted, that served as the only eatery around.

It was late November, and he sat alone with two bites of a large, greasy hamburger, the rest of which sat in his gut like a brick. The bell on the door jingled when she walked in. There was nothing fancy about her that day, or any day for that matter. She wore an oversized, cotton sweater and black wind pants, and her sandy, brown hair was pulled into a messy pony-tail. She was beautiful in a way he had never seen. He wondered if she had just woken up.

They both passed his table and sat down two rows to his left, and he assumed the woman with her was her mother. It was then that he noticed her lips, thin and a pale pink, and it stunned him. He stared too long, as she gave her mother an awkward grin. He glanced away quickly, only to return his gaze a few seconds later. Again, she spotted him. Thankful that he already had his check, he took a last sip of water and headed for the counter.

"Hi," she said after his first two steps. "Do we know each other?"

"Sorry," he replied in a low voice. "You looked familiar. I didn't mean to stare."

That she didn't believe him was all too evident. She introduced him to her mother, Lillian, then revealed her own name: Lucy Tanner.

"Gabriel Alexander," he replied, and shook their hands. "Gabe."

"You from around here, Gabe?" she asked. Her voice was heavy without being masculine.

"Dallas. Student at SMU."

"Major?" her mother asked.

"Journalism. I'm actually headed to Stephenville to interview some landowners for a school assignment. Apparently runoff from neighboring dairies is ruinin' the land." He understood how uninteresting it was as soon as it escaped his mouth, and he couldn't help but smile. "Big news," he said, and they all laughed.

"Enjoy your lunch, ma'am," he said to her mother. "Lucy," he said softly, entranced with the young girl.

She grinned a bit before he walked away, and again he was looking at her lips; they were a perfect shade.

The interviews Gabriel conducted that afternoon were taxing. They were hard, aging people who either had no interest in being interviewed or were so ecstatic to voice their complaints that he rarely got to ask a question. He finished up as the sun was going down, jumped into his car, and headed for the city. *There's something about this part of Texas*, he thought to himself. The homes were small, old, and most in need of repair. He wondered about the people inside. Were they happier here? "Life is just life," he said over the radio. "No matter where you are."

Two hours later, he was re-entering his dorm. He never did get used to the smell. It wasn't his fault; he and his roommate were uncommonly tidy for single, college-age males. It was the building, or perhaps the dark, red carpet covering the floor—worn and long past its useful age—that emitted a permanent odor. The message machine was blinking, one new message.

"Gabe, hi, uh ... I hope it's okay. I called the school and got your number." He knew the voice right away. It was the girl from the diner. Lucy Tanner.

"Anyway, uh ... I didn't know if you might be back in the area anytime soon. I'm staying with my parents for a while. So, I guess, call me if you want." He heard rustling as she went to hang up the phone. "Oh, it's Lucy, from today."

It was an inconvenience that she had forgotten to leave her number. It angered him; he desperately wanted to talk with her again. He sat on the edge of his twin bed, phone in hand, and thought of what to do next. It was a small town. Surely the number of people with her last name would amount to a manageable call list. He grabbed paper and a pen from the desk in the corner of the room, returned to the bed, and dialed information. The third number produced a familiar voice. It was Lucy's mother.

"Is Lucy available?"

"May I tell her who's calling?"

"It's Gabriel, from lunch today," he responded with some embarrassment.

"Ah, the reporter. How'd the interviews go?" she asked.

"Thrilling," he said with heavy sarcasm. She laughed, told him to hold on, and soon Lucy's voice came through.

"Hi there," she said softly. Gabriel's arms shook.

"You made it hard on me," he said.

"I did?"

"You didn't leave your number."

She sighed. "I'm sorry. It's interesting that you found me."

"Is it?"

"I think it is. Tell me something about you," she demanded.

"Hmm. Pizza is my favorite food," he said after a moment. It sounded ridiculous.

"Mine too."

This awkward, meaningless conversation would initiate the most amazing period of Gabriel's life to that point. He would soon care about someone in a way he hadn't known existed, a way that opens a person to a full breadth of joy, pain, and torment. He was already feeling, well, strange. It was strange, in fact, for him to be feeling anything at all. The girls in Gabriel's past had produced no such feeling. He had found them mindless and completely uninteresting.

While I'm Still Myself

Once aware of his indifference to the female population, at least the portion he had encountered, Gabriel told himself that the problem was his own. He vowed to have more patience, to give the next one a chance. The endeavor succeeded only in turning a two-day relationship into two months of misery with a wealthy blonde from Galveston. And now there was Lucy.

They made plans for the following day. Gabriel would drive down and meet her father—the thought of which unnerved him—then they would see a movie. After hanging up the phone, he sat still for several minutes trying to figure out what was happening. Was he ill? It felt as if the blood flowing through his body had been replaced with some foreign substance. He was edgy, nervous, and unable to think clearly. Gabriel glanced at the clock—9:30. "Close enough," he told himself. All he wanted was tomorrow.

The drive down Highway 377 was now slightly familiar. Gabriel enjoyed the stretches of fence and pasture, broken intermittently by a small town, reappearing as the road headed south until finally curving into Bluff Dale. He pulled up to an average-size frame house with two cars parked out front. The address matched what Lucy had given him, so he turned off the car, checked himself in the rearview mirror, and made his way to the door. He wasn't sure if he preferred Lucy or her parents to answer. Both thoughts made him nervous. Gabriel knocked lightly and was greeted by her mother.

"Hello again," she said with a smile. "C'mon in."

The house was older, well kept, and it had a nice smell. Lucy stood in the kitchen next to a tall, thin man. They both watched him; Lucy with a grin and he without. She looked much as she had the day before, but with a tight-knit sweater and faded jeans. The shape of her body was perfect, as he saw it, and he did his best not to stare. She motioned him in with a slight nod. Feeling stiff and uncomfortable in his walk, Gabriel offered a shaky hand to her father.

"Gabriel," he said in a low voice.

His response, "Sir," sounded like a ten-year-old in contrast.

"So, where you kids headed this evenin'?" he asked, in a slightly louder tone.

"Uh, to the movies, I think, if that's all right." Lucy let out a snort of laughter and looked down.

"All right by me," he said. Y'all be safe."

They would laugh about that moment when they got in the car, and several times after. The evening passed far quicker than Gabriel wanted it to, they said good-bye, he kissed her on the cheek, and the phone was ringing the second he stepped back into his dorm two hours later. So began three weeks of two people's complete attachment to one another. They saw each other nearly every day during this time, and when apart, they spent hours on the phone. Gabriel and Lucy laughed and talked then laughed some more. But mostly, they drove. They drove what must have been every back road within one hundred miles of Bluff Dale. The two of them would stop, kiss without breathing, then drive some more. Gabriel was so completely enamored with Lucy Tanner that he all but forgot about his classes and received a rather firm lecture from his mother after not calling home for a week.

He was in love with her but hadn't considered the idea until an afternoon in late December. The phone rang as he was preparing for the drive to her house; he snatched it up after one ring and said hello.

"Gabe, hey," she said. Her voice was different, low and raspy, and her words came slowly.

"Hi. You okay?"

"Yeah. Listen, just meet me at the diner instead of coming to my house." Her words melted together, as though she were talking in her sleep.

"All right, I can do that. You sure you're okay?"

"Yeah, see you in a bit."

Something was wrong, but Gabriel didn't know what. *Is she going to end it?* The thought made his stomach turn; he felt the urge to vomit. After getting ready in a rush he headed for Bluff Dale as he had done nearly every day of the last three weeks, only this time he drove faster and without admiring the countryside. Gabriel didn't notice how tightly he was gripping the wheel until he pulled into the cafe parking lot. His hand ached.

She was sitting with her arms crossed. She looked cold. Her face was different, he thought. Not the face itself, but the person behind it.

"Hi," she said, looking at him with glassy eyes.

Gabriel felt he was meeting a stranger.

"Hi." He wasn't sure what was scaring him, yet the fear was more intense that he had ever experienced.

"I'm a drug addict, Gabe," she said suddenly. "Since I was thirteen. The day you saw me, here, was my second day home from rehab." Her words, and the way she spoke them, sliced through him like razor blades. He knew nothing but to look at her. "Not my first try, by the way," she added with a forced smile.

"What kind?" he asked.

"Pills."

"Pills? What kind of pills?"

"Every kind." She was twisting a napkin.

Understanding his own ignorance on the subject, he leaned back in his chair.

"Okay."

The cafe was silent except for the faint sound of Merle Haggard coming from a radio in the kitchen.

"Can I assume you've taken something? You're not yourself."

She leaned forward and brought their faces together. He felt her breath. "That's just it, sweet boy. I am myself, right now."

"No," he said, shaking his head.

"Gabe, this is me. This is me, and I won't be good for you."

"Stop talking like that," he snapped.

"I will ruin your life. I swear it. I've done it many times. I promise you."

She quickly rose from her chair, placed both hands on his face, and kissed his forehead. Her lips felt frozen on his skin.

"You made me want to do the right thing so bad," she said. "You made me not myself. It was so nice. Thank you."

And she was gone.

Gabriel thought about that moment every day that followed. *I should have followed her*, he thought continually. *I should have told her that I loved her.* He called her house several times in the weeks that followed, but the call was never returned. Gabriel told himself, believing it completely, that she wouldn't call because she loved him.

He didn't learn of her death until after the funeral. A letter arrived in late January with no return address, and when he opened it, he found two small pieces of paper. The first was a newspaper clipping; it was

While I'm Still Myself

Lucy's obituary. Her lips were beautiful even in black and white. The second was a note:

> Gabriel,
> I wanted to write you a short note while I'm still myself and can remember to breathe in and out. Thank you for making her smile again. Her father and I had nearly forgotten how beautiful it was. I hope you do great things.
>
> Lillian Tanner

Gabriel never once noticed the cold that December. The sun refused to shine, but it didn't matter. Everything felt to him just as it should have been. Sitting on a cold, metal bench, a shiver runs through him, and he buries deeper into his coat. A passing cloud allows a hint of light to touch Lucy's headstone, and a thought comes to his mind: *I never got to see her face in the sunshine. It's a shame. I bet it would have been amazing.*

The Guest

"Young man?"

The words floated into the back of his mind, barely registering, as he trudged down the cold hallway of the hospital. The second time it stopped him.

"Young man?"

Clark, in his exhaustion, peered up at the clock on the wall. He had now gone thirty-two hours without sleep. His scalp tingled, and his mind came and went like the beam from a lighthouse. He turned, sipping coffee from a Styrofoam cup, and walked slowly toward an open room on his right.

In the exact center of the room sat a silver-haired woman, covered to the waist with a quilt, her hands resting primly on her lap. "Oh, young man," she said, waving to him with one arm. "I'd like to order some room service. I was hopin' you might save me from botherin' with the phone. Do you mind?"

Clark stood silent. "Uh, well, I ..." he stammered.

"A sandwich, ham on wheat, if you could. Oh, and some lemonade. Gosh, lemonade sounds good, doesn't it?"

Clark turned in time to see a young nurse, blonde and dressed in blue scrubs, exiting a few doors down. "One moment," he said, and then went after the nurse. He did his best to explain the request to her as she smiled knowingly.

"I'll get the sandwich," she said when he was done.

"And the lemonade?"

"Yes, and the lemonade."

He reappeared in the doorway and with a smile said, "Your order is in, ma'am. Your food should be here shortly." Before he could turn to leave, she waved to him again. "Why don't you come in? Have a seat." Clark bought time with another sip of coffee then stepped in hesitantly. He sat gently in a brown vinyl chair just inside the door and crossed one leg over the other.

"How long have you worked at this inn?" she asked, a frown forming in anticipation of the answer.

"Well, actually, I—"

"It's not bad, this one. A bit plain, a little cold, but nice enough," she said, interrupting him. Clark nodded and took another sip.

Not the nicest I've seen, though," she continued. "When I was a girl, my father took me to New Orleans. I was only five, but I can still see it like it was yesterday." She clutched her chest with one hand, gave a half-smile, and shook her head gently. "What a place—giant white columns all along the front and the most amazing chandeliers all over. Every bellhop dressed for a ball." She narrowed her eyes at him and learned forward. "More than I can say for you, mister."

"I'm off duty," Clark replied with a grin. "My wife just had a baby."

Her eyes widened with delight as she took a long breath. "Congratulations, sir. How incredibly exciting. The name?"

"A girl," he said proudly. "Daisy."

She became visibly excited, her motions more animated.

"I love the name Daisy. My best friend growin' up, her name was Daisy. I was always envious of her name. I tried to buy it, trade for it, all kindsa nonsense. Never worked."

"And what's the name you were in such a hurry to get rid of?" Clark asked.

"Emelia," she responded, offering her hand.

He leaned forward and shook her hand gently. "Nice to meet you, Emelia. I'm Clark. And I don't think you should have been trying to trade that name away. It's lovely."

Her cheeks flushed red, and she looked away.

"Clark, before you go, could you do me one more favor?"

He nodded and set his cup down on the floor next to him. "Of course."

"Could you put some fresh water in these flowers?" she asked, pointing toward a narrow wooden table beside the hospital bed, where sat a clear, hourglass-shaped vase with bright yellow tulips. "I always leave them for the next guests. Somethin' I've done all my life and plan to keep doin' while I'm still myself."

Clark rose, filled a cup with water from the sink, and walked over to fill the vase. He noticed a five-by-seven picture frame propped against the wall. It held a photo, black and white, of a young girl leaning into a middle-aged man. They looked at each other rather than the camera.

"My father and me," she said, noticing his stare.

She was young, six or seven he guessed, wearing a cotton dress to the ankles and no shoes. Her father, squatting next to her, appeared tall and thin, suspenders draped over a button-down shirt. His hair was dark, healthy, and manicured. They shared the same nose.

"Great picture," Clark said after a few seconds.

She sighed. "To think, I was once someone's little girl. Amazing, isn't it. It all goes away so fast. People, time, life ... so fast."

He turned to look at her. Her hair, long and healthy in the photo, was now white and brittle. Her skin was thin, like a water balloon, the blood coursing just below the surface. Her eyes were the same, he thought to himself. Perfectly white around a blue center. "Great picture," he said again. "I better be going."

"Thank you for your help," she said, nodding.

"Enjoy your stay, Emelia."

"I will. I have. Thank you, Clark." He turned and headed for the door. "Make sure the next guest gets my flowers," she said as he left the room.

On his way to the elevator, Clark passed a nurse pushing a food cart and spotted a sandwich, made with wheat bread, resting next to a glass of lemonade. He rode to the second floor, where in the last room of a long corridor he found his wife awake.

"There you are," she said, with a tilt of her head. He walked over to his new daughter and, careful not to wake her, touched one finger to the top of her head.

———

The closing of a door woke Clark from an awkwardly positioned sleep. He sat forward, rubbed his eyes, and was surprised to find the clock showing that three hours had passed since he sat down. A nurse peeked at the baby and walked over to tend to his wife.

"Looks like we're gonna get you a more comfortable room," she whispered. "Maybe your husband can get some rest."

Clark followed as his wife and baby were wheeled to the elevator, down to a different floor, and into a new room. He was the last to enter, and after setting down his bags, he walked over to have another look at his new daughter. Just before he reached her, something caught the corner of his eye. There, on a table next to the bed, sat a clear vase filled with yellow tulips, one wilted petal having fallen to the ground.

The Reflection, Only Hers

As a toddler, healthy and gorgeous with curly, blonde hair and cream-colored eyes, Annabel Shay would roam about the house, ignoring everything bought for her, and find a corner, a bag, a cranny of any kind and begin to rip everything from the location in order to see what the inner workings might teach her. This was a constant bother to her parents, Jack and Millie. Yet in between the warnings and the swats on the hand, Jack would marvel at her unending curiosity, it being more than he'd ever seen, and he would wonder how this characteristic would manifest itself in the later life of his beautiful daughter.

At the end of a day, after Annabel had been placed in her crib and covered with kisses and the amount of blankets proper for the season, Jack and Millie would collapse into the couch in pure exhaustion. One would give a chuckle, remembering something little Annabel had done, a face she had made, and the other would laugh for the same incident, or perhaps another. Yet other times, as Jack Shay sat alone with a glass of bourbon or a cigar, or both, it was the curiosity of his daughter that crept into his thoughts. Jack knew curiosity had killed some kitten somewhere and at some point in time, and though he didn't pretend to know the details of that story, it remained true that what had been a problem for that kitten could just as well become a problem for his precious daughter. He would sip his bourbon until the fears subsided.

Jack watched his daughter grow into a young lady, now twelve years old, that period of time between childhood and womanhood, with only the occasional incident. Once, at church, Annabel and a couple of easily persuaded friends snuck out of their Bible class, their teacher having stepped out of the room for only a moment, and ambled down to a healthy garden out behind the old church storage shed. The bright red of a ripe tomato caught Annabel's attention, and she picked it to have a closer look. Her mind wandered from the beauty of this round wonder of nature to its undeniable baseball-like shape, and having set her mind, she wheeled around and launched it back up toward the building at the head of Johnny Wheeler.

Little Johnny, awkward and uncomfortable in the role of a dropout, stood with his arms crossed, talking to Sadie Brooke, and without warning, the bigger-than-average tomato made contact with the bridge of Johnny's nose and exploded in every direction. Johnny was sent reeling back onto his rear, and Sadie stood in horror, looking down at her ruined dress. Annabel, secretly proud of her impeccable aim, stood and awaited a reaction. Then, as if a corpse resurrected, Johnny Wheeler sat upright, tomato seeds covering every inch of his face, and the three of them burst into a thundering simultaneous laughter. Later, as Jack Shay escorted his daughter through the sea of amused onlookers, Johnny leaned into Annabel and whispered, "Hell of an arm on you, Shay." Her only reaction was a thin smile, and they loaded into the family Ford and quickly drove away.

As Annabel was growing up, her mother, Millie Shay, was growing worse. Millie was an incredible specimen, tall and beautiful throughout her life, with a wonderfully kind heart that made her well liked among all who knew her. This, along with the money—first from her own family, and later from a successful husband—made it seem as if Millie's life was near to perfect. Things were not perfect, however, though both she and Jack did their best to conceal the fact from others. Millie Shay was the victim of genetics. Her mind was not quite right, leading her to have "issues," as the people in Bluff Dale would refer to it whenever a discussion about her took place. She was prone to depression, anxiety, heavy drinking, and most severe were the instances when she would see things and people that were not there.

Millie was often hospitalized during Annabel's young adulthood. Jack had become very good at sweetening the situation whenever his precious Annabel asked about it, often saying simply, "Your mother is just a little bit sick. These doctors haven't figured it out just yet, so they're tryin' again." Jack, surprising even himself with how innocent it all sounded, would hug his daughter and encourage her to worry about other things. At these times he felt like a wooden doll, doing only what was expected of him at the pull of a string, knowing in his heart that neither he nor his daughter could be shielded to any great degree.

Millie Shay's first trip to the state hospital had been a quiet one, kept away from the rest of the small town, with Jack being the only witness to her breakdown. The second, however, was in full view of young Annabel and made quite an impression on her despite all the efforts of her loving father. Millie, having been in the fourth consecutive day of consistent drinking, became certain she was being attacked. After flailing about in the front yard grass, she was restrained by her husband while screams echoed off the trees surrounding the Shay house. Annabel, watching from the corner of the yard, stood perfectly still as Jack calmed Millie then escorted her gently into the house.

It was following this event that Annabel began to search out information for herself and to do her own studying about the behavior displayed by the lovely Mrs. Shay. Through a combination of stealing her mother's medical papers and long hours at the school library, Annabel became incredibly well educated on conditions such as schizophrenia, depression, and alcoholism. She let Jack know none of what she had done or had come to know and instead allowed him to shield her from the problem whenever he felt the need.

Annabel was not ignorant to the situation, however, and in fact had set herself to pondering what exactly should be done about things. It had become her judgment that first, due to the seemingly hereditary nature of the diseases from which Millie suffered, it was inevitable that Annabel would begin to show signs of the same problems at some point in her life. Second, with that said, it was imperative that she discover what the world could teach her before it was too late—before she was no longer herself.

These conclusions led her down to the creek on a frigid January morning in 1957. Annabel was fifteen, as was Johnny Wheeler, her companion on that morning, and the two of them trudged through the brittle winter grass, snapping frozen branches off of trees as they went down to the old Bluff Dale creek. The water was frozen in shallow areas and in some spots near the bank, but it wasn't the creek they were interested in at all. They had come to seek out the train tracks that ran alongside the water for about a mile and a half before the tracks darted north, and the two separated forever.

"I think I left it over here somewhere," said Annabel, pointing toward a brushy patch along some trees.

Johnny, having been completely in love with Annabel for several years now, followed behind her like a most loyal dog. The thing she was referring to—and had hidden in the brush—was an average-size green suitcase filled with enough clothes for one week, the necessary tooth and hair brush, a notepad, pen, and thirty-eight dollars saved from her last three birthdays. Annabel brushed the leaves and grass from the top of the suitcase and pulled it up to her side.

"You sure this is a good idea, Anna?" asked Johnny sheepishly. "Your parents are gonna be awfully upset."

Annabel turned to face him and after stomping her foot down with authority, gave a stern reply. "Johnny Wheeler, I didn't tell you about this so you could whine and cry and try to talk me out of it. I'm not gonna sit around and wait to go crazy like my poor mother. I gotta see things in this world. I wanna live. Go places. While I'm still myself and can make things happen."

The young boy watched his own foot as he kicked a rock down into the water. "We're just gonna miss ya round here is all." The sadness in his voice wouldn't allow Annabel to be angry at him. She placed her hand softly on his shoulder. "I'll be back one of these days, John boy."

He responded only with a slight nod, and the two of them headed farther into the woods, staying beside the river until they came to a shallow spot where the creek could easily be crossed. Three long strides placed Annabel on the opposite bank, with Johnny not far behind. They stood for a moment, and Annabel caught the smell of rain. The two of them examined the large black clouds moving in from the west then trudged on up the embankment where the ground leveled out and the train tracks could be seen thirty yards to the east. Annabel, with legs scraped from briars and brush, made her way toward the tracks.

"Maybe the train ain't comin' today," Johnny said from behind her. Annabel looked down at her watch. It was simple, trimmed in gold, with a black wristband. It was a gift from her father, given on her thirteenth birthday, and she treasured it more than anything else she owned. She cleaned a smudge from the glass with the sleeve of her shirt.

"Train comes every mornin' at eight thirty. It's just now eight twenty."

The two of them sat down on the track, Annabel's suitcase separating them, and listened to the distant roll of thunder. Annabel, so fiercely confident of her decision in response to Johnny's question, began to consider the implications of what she was about to do. Her mother, so fragile already, would fall apart when her daughter left. Annabel wondered if it would be the final straw, the culminating event that sent her off the deep end forever. She thought of her father, the saint, the man who so many times had calmed her after a tragedy; the man who repeatedly nursed her mother back to health. He would be devastated, she thought to herself, but he would understand.

The tracks began to gently vibrate under them, and at once they both stood up. The soft hiss of a train was barely audible as Annabel looked down at her watch.

"Told ya, Johnny. Eight thirty. Every day."

"I'm goin' with ya," he said suddenly. "I'm goin' with ya."

"You'll do no such thing!" she said loudly. Then in a calmer voice she added, "You know you can't do that. You know it."

Annabel felt a lump rise in her throat, and her eyes began to fill. She grabbed him by the arm, and with the train growing louder and coming closer, the two of them jogged down behind a large oak tree and hid behind it. The train was approaching now, and just as Annabel predicted in her own mind, she heard the train begin to slow a bit. She wasn't sure why, but when the train passed through this part of the woods it always slowed just a bit, and this would allow her the chance to catch the ride she had been planning for several weeks. Annabel dropped the suitcase on the ground beside her and wrapped both arms around Johnny Wheeler. "Bye, Johnny," she said softly.

The train was now in view rounding the corner, and in a flash the conductor car had passed, followed by a sea of rusty yellow cars. Annabel waited for an open one to come around, as it always did, and at last one appeared. She let go of Johnny and reached down for her suitcase.

He grabbed her arm and yelled, "Anna."

She pulled from him, he had a surprisingly strong grip, and in a desperate measure she lunged out and pushed him to the ground. In a flash, she was running, green suitcase in hand, toward the tracks and her open car. The train had now slowed considerably, and as the car approached, Annabel slung her suitcase in. Then, running beside it until she caught her top speed, she jumped up onto a step, grabbed the handrail, and pulled herself in. Peeking out, she was able to catch one last glimpse of Johnny Wheeler before the train car moved on into the trees. Annabel moved to the corner of the car, out of the sight of the world, and sat down.

———————

A few miles away stood Jack Shay, his breath fogging on the cold glass of a living room window, his daughter's neatly folded bed on his mind. He glanced back at a photo of Annabel that hung above the mantel, his moist eyes blurring it beyond recognition, then back toward the rain clouds forming in the west.

———————————

Three hours later, Annabel lay shivering on the cold metal floor of the train car. The sun burned brightly in the sky, illuminating the passing outside world, but it had yet to remove the chill lodged deep in her bones. Using two folded shirts as pillows and another as covering, she forced herself to close her eyes. She drifted off to sleep as the miles separated her from everything she had known. Annabel, normally a light sleeper unable to take daytime naps, slept soundly for nearly five hours. She awoke feeling disoriented and at first unsure of where she was. The steady clicking of the tracks was an instant reminder. She sat up, rubbed her eyes, and began to try to stand up.

"Hello there!"

The voice sent Annabel backward and down on her backside. The corners of the car were dark, but she could make out the silhouette of a man, covered in shadow, with only his teeth visible. He was clearly smiling.

"What … how … who are you?" she uttered nervously.

The man rose, steadied himself against the back wall of the train car, and began making his way toward her slowly with his hand out. Annabel retreated farther into her corner, and the man put both hands out, palms facing her, gesturing that he meant her no harm.

"Name's Burt. Burt Cottle. The few friends I've got call me Rocky. Glad to see ya movin' round now. You sure were lyin' still over there. Had me worried you was a goner," he said with a joking smile.

He had moved into the light, allowing Annabel to better inspect his appearance. He was homeless, or looked to be, at the very least. His hair was equal parts red and gray, disheveled and brittle rather than greasy, and an unkempt beard covered the majority of his face. His eyes were jet black, deep set, and warm. Despite his questionable hygiene, Annabel could not argue that he had planned for the weather better than she had. His boots were worn but still in decent condition, and his dark blue pants sported only a few small holes. She envied his coat. It was black, or had been at one time, and despite being a bit dusty, it was in good shape. She cursed herself for not bringing one of her own.

"I'm Annabel. How did you get on this train?" she asked.

"Been meanin' to take this ride for a while. Just now gettin' round to it. Jumped aboard just outside of Childress. Little town called Tell. Ever been there?"

Annabel shook her head. "No. Never."

"Ain't missin' much," he said, with a wheezing laugh. "Post office and a couple'a houses. Train stops just outside of town there ever once in a while."

"Hmm," she said. A few seconds passed, and she added, "Well, where ya goin'?"

"Amarilla," he said, pointing in the wrong direction. "Got somebody I need to visit. How 'bout you?"

Annabel scratched her elbow. Looking down at her feet, she said softly, "Not sure exactly. Just wanna see some things. Go places."

She looked up at him to study his reaction and found that he was studying her as well. His eyes narrowed as he contemplated her.

"You're awful young to be out on your own, Annabel. Somethin' happen? Somebody treat ya wrong back at home?"

"No. Nothing like that," she said, sitting back down next to her suitcase. "I'd rather not discuss it."

"No problem," he said, and turned back toward his corner.

He walked over, reached into the dark, and when he returned to the light he held a worn duffle bag at his side. "Mind if I sat near ya? Tough to hear over tha noise of this train. And my hearin' certainly ain't what it used to be."

She didn't respond, but moved her suitcase from one side to the other, and he took it as an invitation. He sat down slowly, as if allowing his bones time to adjust, but once seated he assumed an Indian-style position, like an eager child. He then pulled the duffle bag out into full view.

"Whatcha got in your bag?" he asked with a youth-like exuberance.

Annabel shrugged and ran her hand over the green suitcase. "Nothin' much. Just some clothes. Toothbrush. Pen and paper."

He straightened his back and raised his eyebrows as if impressed. "Ah! A writer, eh? Never much good at it myself. Never liked readin' either, really. Got any poems? Now poems I like."

"Nah," she said quietly. "It's for letters. Gotta write my daddy to let him know I'm all right."

His face tightened at the sadness in her tone. A few seconds passed before he decided not to press her on the issue.

Finally, Annabel sat up and pointed toward his bag. "What's in yours?"

He grabbed it, as if she would never ask, and loosed the string at the top. "Well, let's see here," he mumbled while rummaging through. "Coupl'a shirts. Both need washin.' Pair a socks. Aha!" he said loudly and removed a half-empty bottle of bourbon with no label. His smile dissipated as he thought it over, and he shoved it back into the bag.

"Probably not of interest to you. Wait, here's somethin.' You play cards?" He removed a deck of playing cards, all edges worn, with a rubber band creasing the middle as it held them together. He removed the band and began filing through as if warming them up.

"Go Fish," said Annabel with a shrug. "That's about it."

His face once again became animated with excitement. "One a the greatest of card games. Although,

I must warn ya, I'm tough to beat. Care to give it a go?" It was late afternoon, and Annabel finally managed her first thin smile of the day. She angled herself slightly toward her new traveling companion and awaited her allotment of cards.

The tournament lasted four rounds, all being tightly contested, with Annabel winning every game. After a sportsman's handshake, Burt Cottle wrapped up his cards and dropped them back into the duffle bag. He stood, slowly again, and ambled his way toward the open door of the train car. He peered out at the passing countryside, first one direction then the other, and turned to Annabel with a nod. "Not far outta' Amarilla' now. Maybe another half hour," he said confidently. "Say, why don't ya jump off with me when we get there? Just to stretch your legs a bit. Be good for you to get outta here for a few. You can jump the next train if ya like."

The idea didn't sound bad to Annabel. The constant noise had begun to numb her head, and she was hungry.

"Long as we can get somethin' to eat," she replied. "I'm 'bout to starve."

"Whatever you like, Miss Annabel," said the old vagabond. "Whatever you like."

Annabel and Mr. Cottle sat against the metal car, in the middle now, and watched as the countryside gradually changed in favor of civilization. Houses began appearing in the distance, sparsely at first, then in clumps of neighborhoods on the outskirts of Amarillo. The train then began a slow climb, and Annabel crawled toward the opening to watch as trees, power lines, and houses moved farther away. She felt the pace of the train slowing gradually, and at last it came to a complete stop. Annabel rose to her feet and turned to find Burt, already standing, with her suitcase in his hand and the black bag over his shoulder.

"Here ya are, ma'am," he said with a smile.

She returned the smile and took the suitcase from him. "Thank ya kindly, sir."

Annabel suddenly felt invigorated, brimming with nervousness and anticipation. Her mother's problems, the very fears causing her to flee, now seemed a world away. The two of them stepped down from the train car and onto rocky ground. They stood on the side of a mountain, or at least what seemed like a mountain to a young girl, and could see the entire town of Amarillo spread over the land like butter, thinly in some spots, clumpy and condensed in others. She watched as cars moved silently down one street and then another. Some were dull, like most where she was from, but others were shiny and elegant with the setting sun bouncing off them as they drove.

"Well," said Burt, "let's get ya somethin' to eat."

The two of them moved down the embankment, the incline forcing them into a jog, until they reached street level. Annabel marveled at the dark-red brick covering most of the road. She considered how different this town was from Bluff Dale, where the roads were dust and gravel, with only the main highway covered in a mundane blacktop. Homes of all sizes lined the streets in both directions, most good sized but ill manicured, with three or four large columns along the front porches. The lawns were sparse, browned from the abuse of winter, the trees leafless and gray. Still, for Annabel, it was enchanting. They headed west until they came to an intersection.

To continue west on Dow Street, as the sign indicated, seemed less interesting than heading into the heart of town. After two blocks, the houses began to give way to service stations, restaurants, and a thrift store in the bottom of a two-story building. She could see the odds and ends scattered through the window and watched as the lights went out and the sign rotated from open to closed. She gazed up to the second floor, where the windows sat filthy and covered in dust. From her view, the place showed no activity, no sign of inhabitance, and she considered to herself that finding a warm place to sleep for the night would be necessary. Her thoughts were interrupted by a soft tap on the arm.

"Bet we can get a bite to eat right up there, Miss Annabel," said Burt, pointing up and to the left.

The building was white, perfectly square, except for a large dome structure protruding up from the middle. Though it was a block away, she could make out the letters painted across the front: Maria's Mexican Cantina.

"Tacos sure sound good, don't they?" she replied. "I could eat fifty of 'em."

The two companions made their way for another block, still walking on the impressive red brick, then across the small parking lot until they approached the dome. It appeared exaggerated, unnecessary when compared to everything else on the street. She watched as it disappeared above her upon entering the restaurant.

Once inside, the smell of warm food assaulted Annabel's nose, and she became nearly faint with hunger. The interior of the building was cut exactly in half with a large blue wall separating the dining area from the kitchen. A laminated sign posted above them indicated that they should seat themselves, and they quickly sat down at the nearest table. Annabel set the suitcase down next to her, and Burt, sitting across from her, did the same with his black duffle bag. Scanning the room, she exchanged glances with a young man in the far corner, his hair a mess, axel grease smeared on his forearm, as he sipped from a near-empty beer mug. From the side approached a short, overweight Hispanic woman, her black hair pulled tightly into a bun, a large stain across her bosom, carrying a platter with only a glass of melted ice and a wet rag.

"I be right back," she said as she passed the table. Her accent was heavy, and Annabel noticed bright-pink lipstick attached to her front teeth as she smiled.

Annabel nodded, glanced again at the man in the corner, now paying attention to only the last of his beer, and returned her attention to her new friend.

"So," she said, shifting in her seat, "why Rocky?"

Mr. Cottle tilted his head upward as if to see her from a different angle. "Pardon?"

"When we first met," she insisted, "you told me your friends call you Rocky. Why?"

He nodded in understanding. "Oh, yes. Well, ya see, I had a bit of a temper in my younger years. Got in a few scrapes here and there." He looked away and shrugged with embarrassment. "Quite a few, actually. Tha boys went ta callin' me Rocky, after Rocky Marciano. Name latched on, I guess."

Annabel sensed it was a story told with pride when talking with a man, but with her he seemed ashamed, embarrassed at the barbaric nature of it all. She changed the subject for his benefit, and pleasant conversation carried them through to their meal. They soon found they had ordered far more than they could eat. Annabel paid the check with folded money that sat inside an envelope, which sat inside the green suitcase, and the two of them made for the door. Just before leaving, Annabel stopped and approached the waitress. The lipstick still clung to her front teeth.

"Yes," she said, smiling. "What I can do for you?"

Annabel took a quick peek to her left and right before speaking. "Yes. I was wonderin,'" she said as she smoothed out her dress, "is there any chance you folks could use some help in here? I mean, I could learn anything, and I work hard."

The waitress's eyes narrowed, and she began to size Annabel up, looking first at her face, then down to her legs, and back up again. She nodded sideways and asked, "Who you talking to in there?"

"Oh," she said with a laugh, "that's just Mr. Cottle. I know he don't dress fancy, but he's real nice. Just met him today, but he's real nice."

The waitress sized her up again, head to toe, and at once her face softened. "You talk to my brother. He owns restaurant. He come at seven tomorrow."

"Seven tomorrow? Oh, thank you. I'll be here in the morning, then."

The waitress nodded politely, and Annabel made for the exit. The breeze, now much cooler in the last bit of daylight, raised the hair on her neck. She covered her chest with one arm, the other still holding the suitcase, and walked quickly toward Burt as he stood near the road.

"Did ya forget somethin,'" he asked as she approached.

"No," she said, looking back in the direction they had come from. "I'm gonna talk to the owner about a job there tomorrow."

"A job, huh?" he said, seemingly impressed. "Guess you plan on stickin' around here a bit, then."

"Maybe. We'll see."

Annabel's attention was focused back on the two-story building that housed the thrift store. She began walking down the street, toward the building, and she felt Burt following behind.

She shivered as she gazed over the building from across the street. There was no one there as far as she could tell, and the only sign of life was a dim light in the back of the thrift store. It seemed to her the kind of light someone left on at all times. She exhaled through pursed lips.

"Whatcha thinkin,' Miss Annabel?" Burt asked.

"I'm thinkin' I gotta save my money. I don't have enough to be rentin' a room to sleep in."

"You wanna sleep in there?" he asked after a moment.

Annabel shrugged. "Don't see any harm in it. I don't think there's a soul up there." She pointed to the windows about the store. Her friend didn't respond. "C'mon," she said, taking her first step to cross the road. Annabel looked in all directions to see who might be watching, and when she was sure there was no one, she picked up her pace and walked along the sidewall.

The lot behind the building held nothing, save two metal trashcans brimming with full garbage bags and flies, and an old, rusted car fender propped against the back fence.

"Now, I'm not sure..." Burt said as she made her way up the concrete steps and approached the back door.

"Shh!" she said with a frown, pressing one finger against her lips.

The wooden door was unpainted, splintered at the bottom, and looked generally rotten. Annabel considered the possibility of kicking it a couple of times, but she discovered there was no need as she turned the handle and it opened with a creak. She turned toward Burt, now standing nervously behind her, and opened her eyes wide. He shrugged, and the two of them entered the building, closing the door quietly behind them.

After maneuvering through the thrift store and up the stairs, Annabel stood and looked out across the second floor. It was better than she had expected. Instead of cold, hard floor, they found two dusty couches, both black somewhere under the layers of dirt, a lamp with a navy blue shade, and some old paintings leaned up against the corner wall. A large, cracked mirror hung in the exact middle of the back wall. She nodded in surprised approval and then turned to Burt. "A lot better than sleepin' in the street, wouldn't ya say?"

He no longer looked nervous and was now smiling. "Sure is," he said with a wide grin.

The two of them strolled in, and after wandering around the room and looking briefly out of each window, they made themselves at home. There wasn't much to it, really, other than setting their bags down out of the way and finding a place for the night. Annabel, before allowing anyone to sit, took the cushions from the couches and gave each its own thorough beating. Dust clouded the room when she was done, but they now had a decent place to sit and sleep.

Annabel, concerned about her appearance after the day's adventure, strolled over to the cracked mirror and stood in front. Her hair was tossed but still presentable, and her legs showed the signs of a walk through the brush. Her eyes caught a glimpse of a thread, frayed and broken, just behind the collar of her knee-length dress. "Burt," she said, grasping at the thread, "Burt, could you come over and tell me if my dress is ripped? I can't really see it." She heard no footsteps, and after a moment, turned to him. "Burt?"

He remained sitting and eyed her with a concerned look.

"Do you mind?" she asked again.

He stood slowly, as if pondering each movement, and began walking slowly toward her. Before he reached her he said, "I hate to tell you, Miss Annabel, but that dress is ruined." He stood behind her. She felt his breath, his presence, but the mirror showed only her reflection. "I'm sorry about your dress," he said. "Sorry indeed."

Annabel studied her own face in the mirror for several seconds. Then, understanding completely, she sat down, placed her head in her hands, and wept over a life not yet lived.

The Pebblestone Five

Somewhere along the Texas Panhandle sits a town like most others in that part of the country. A few buildings—mostly boarded up—sit scattered, seemingly by happenstance, among a decaying post office, a filthy, roach-filled corner store, and houses with missing shingles and grass reaching the bottom of the windows. The town's name, though not worth mentioning, is of interest only due to its being derived from a stray dog that, as history tells it, would meander back and forth between the porch of the local watering hole (now nothing more than a rotten frame without roof or walls) and the town post office (not in vastly better condition, but inhabited by a toothless drunkard of a postman known by the name Booger).

Despite the faded, green sign welcoming travelers to the town and displaying the population, it would be easy to assume that the place had long ago been deserted. It could have once been a prosperous farming town or a spot in the road staked out by an aging few, their children having left at the first opportunity. As with most places, however, there was more to this town than could be seen from the highway that ran sadly through the flat, dusty plains and eventually found relief in the mountains of New Mexico and Colorado. There was evil that the civilized world may never have known, and in an unforgettable summer in an utterly forgettable year, there was Ceely Dawn Thomas.

All told, the town held a population of one hundred sixty-two, though even the most regionally savvy citizens struggled to think there were that many people within one hundred miles. The majority of these villagers was nowhere near the town proper, and were instead sprinkled like grass seed along the dusty, narrow county roads and crisscrossing fence lines running east and west from the highway. "Drivin' in," as most called it, was a chore better put off until the most dire of necessity, with most avoiding the corner store in favor of their own pristine, white chicken eggs, homegrown beef, and milk pulled from the udders of skinny livestock with sad eyes.

The west road, accessible only by truck due to the three- and four-foot terraces and crater-like potholes, led past mobile home after mobile home until finally coming to a stop at the gate of Cecil Dowry. Mr. Dowry lived alone, his wife long dead and his children long gone, in a nice home relative to the properties between his and the highway. The west road was for the less privileged—those living on fixed incomes and state assistance—and it showed. Broken toys and disassembled cars littered the grassless lawns surrounding single-wide trailers with the underpinning either damaged or completely gone. Aside from Mr. Dowry, there was only one other west-sider who exhibited any sort of pride in his establishment: Father Brown, the town priest.

Father Brown was a highly respected man of the cloth who, through his own ingenuity, turned an old two-wheel camper into a confession room following the closing of the church in town because of financial problems. The church, in fact, was the utility room of a short-lived eatery, with the financial problems resulting from his eleven parishioners struggling to pay the electricity bill each month. Still, he offered spiritual guidance to any who visited the camper, and his wife, Nelda, routinely cooked her well-known casseroles for visitors.

Ceely Dawn lived on the east side of the highway in the only spot that so much as resembled a neighborhood; four-frame houses equal distance from each other, similar in size and shape, but different in color, with fairly manicured lawns and grass cut to respectable height. Ceely had a friend in each of the other three houses, and on hot summer nights, the four children would travel through their fenceless backyards, across the pasture, and arrive at the only park in the city—thirty square yards of pebblestone, upon which sat six swings attached to a metal frame, and one wobbly merry go-round.

The sun was long hidden, but the heat remained as she exited the back door late one Friday night in July. She was quiet, though she didn't know why. Her mother, known as Dolly to her family and friends, was gone as usual. Exactly where, Ceely wasn't sure, but she was fully aware of her mother's deep desire to socialize with friends of better caliber than could be found within twenty miles of home. At least three nights a week she would be gone deep into the night, and Ceely would pray for her safe arrival before falling asleep.

The reasons for her mother's regular departure were many and varied. For one thing, she had the means. Ceely's grandfather, sheriff of the county and well known throughout the region, had been uncommonly wise with money in his younger years and had for Dolly a substantial sum of money when she turned of age. Through good luck and a few timely investments, Dolly had grown her original sum, and with her only expenses being food, gas, utilities, and vodka, she was able to live off of the accruing interest. The other reason for her constant leaving, and Ceely's perpetual misery, was John Carney.

John Carney was husband to Dolly, stepfather to Ceely Dawn (though she loathed the title and refused to speak the words anywhere or to anyone), and a miserable man of evil tendencies. He was ten years younger than his wife, and despite having held a job at a ranch a few miles west of home, he always managed to spend all of his money and begin dipping into his wife's, she having made the mistake of adding him to her accounts upon their marriage. His expenditures were predictable: poker and the occasional drive to the city for a woman. He did not drink—to his credit—this being the only clean spot on an otherwise filthy character. Ceely avoided him at all costs, prayed for him to be occupied with something other than her, and did her best to never be home alone with him.

Ceely stepped high through the grass, mindful of snakes and briars, as she made her way across the pasture toward the pebblestone. She carried a flashlight in her dress pocket, though it wasn't currently needed due to the full moon beaming overhead. She heard voices at a low murmur, so she picked up her pace. Once she was within twenty yards, give or take, she kneeled down and cupped her hands around her mouth. "Coo, Coo," she called into the cloudless sky, the wind at her back carrying her voice impressively. Four calls of the same nature were returned, as they always were, and she rose to walk the last bit of distance. "Sorry I'm late," she said as she stepped up onto the pebblestone.

Upon the merry-go-round sat Katie Trimmel, ten years old, tall and lanky, with sandy colored hair always pulled into a ponytail. She was Ceely's next-door neighbor, and the two had been friends ever since the Trimmels had, for whatever reason, landed in town a few years back. Ceely knew little of her parents, despite living next to them, but had strong opinions about their worth as human beings.

Katie stood and made her way toward Ceely, the two of them embracing after reaching each other. Behind her came two familiar faces, Little Dave Mackey and Todd Hargrove, both eight years old with crew cuts and bushy eyebrows. Standing a distance away was an unfamiliar silhouette. A boy, she could tell in the moonlight, but smaller than the rest of the group. She guessed five or six at most. "Who's this?" she asked, nodding her head in the young one's direction.

"Jonathan Moseley," replied Little Dave.

The boy went around the rest of the kids and approached Ceely with his hand out. "Go by John," he said professionally. "Sometimes John boy."

Impressed with his manner, she shook his hand and holding back a smile, introduced herself. His eyes were large, round, and seemingly alert, the eyes of one who always felt the need to take in the situation around him. His hair was light and floppy, blown out of place by the slightest breeze, and long enough to touch the freckles surrounding his nose. He wore a mismatched tank top and shorts—typical dress for those not yet consumed with vanity—and a pair of canvas slip-ons.

"Who brought him?" she asked the others, still shaking his hand.

"Me. I did, C," replied Little Dave, his eyebrows raised in anticipation. "Moved in just down tha road from me a few days ago. We got ta' talkin,' and well … "

"Awful young to be sneakin' out," said Ceely. "Could be trouble."

Little Dave cleared his throat, preparing to speak, but John spoke first. "Won't be no trouble. Can't be. Can't be trouble when no one's worried 'bout ya."

"I see," she replied with a nod.

The same could be said for the rest of the children gathered around her. Sneaking out of their homes after midnight had become a regular event for this band of kids. The children were largely ignored—side notes to those tasked with their care—and Ceely had become a sort of mother to all of them, though she herself had just turned fourteen. The pebblestone gatherings consisted of casual talk, each telling the others the goings on of the past week, and encouraging one another in whatever was of current interest. Katie loved to draw. Little Dave and Todd were both avid hunters (though at ten years old this consisted mainly of BB Guns and squirrels), and would talk endlessly about exotic safaris in far-off places, "one of these days." The true reason for the meetings, however, was far less jovial.

"Bring the camera, Katie?" Ceely asked.

"Course," she responded, then made her way to a small bag on the ground propped against one leg of the swing-set frame.

"Ever'body line up," Ceely ordered. Each child did as instructed, with Katie handing over the camera and stepping to the front of the line.

Todd placed one hand on the shoulder of little John Moseley, and leaned into his ear. "'Member, we told you 'bout this part. No need to worry."

The child responded with a confident nod, though the older children imagined his nervousness.

Ceely looked down at him, found his eyes fixed on her, and moved to Katie. "Katie girl," she said with one hand on her hip.

Katie turned, her back facing Ceely, and raised her shirt just below the bra line. In the moonlight, Ceely saw the outline of several long, narrow bruises spanning the width of her back. Ceely put the Polaroid camera to her eye, pushed the button, and the air illuminated like a flash of lightning. Katie pulled her shirt down and turned back toward Ceely. "Belt," she said and looked to the ground.

Little Dave was next. He pulled back one shirt sleeve to show bruises, made by his father, in the shape of an angry hand. He told how he'd been in his room when a drunk Bart Mackey barged in and clamped down on his arm in order to drag him to the family room, the cause of his fury being an empty cup not carried to the sink. Ceely snapped the pictures; the Polaroid spit them out.

She moved to Todd Hargrove, who shook his head. "Lucky this week, C."

While I'm Still Myself

At the end of the line stood the new member, John Moseley. Ceely leaned down to his eye level, narrowed her eyes, and offered a calming grin.

He didn't return it. Instead, he nodded once and inserted two fingers into the inside of his left cheek and stretched his lip out. Ceely reached for her flashlight, turned it on, and looked closer to find an open wound, healing but still inflamed. She set her flashlight down and snapped two pictures as the other children shifted angles in order to get a look. She continued to look at him after lowering the camera, his eyes glistening in the moonlight and hair flopping in the breeze, until he spoke. "Back a tha hand. Couple'a days ago. Barely can see the bruise on the outside anymore."

The newly taken photos were placed and stacked with the others inside Katie's bag, along with the camera. The children said their good-byes and made plans to meet again in two days. Katie, the bag slung over one shoulder, strode toward her home, with Todd following behind her. Ceely once again knelt down in front of John boy.

"Both your parents live with you?" she asked.
"Yep."

"How's your mom treat you?"

"Don't see her much. She's away a lot," he responded.

"Got other family?" Ceely asked.

"My grandparents live near Dallas. I don't get to visit them much, but they're real nice."

Ceely nodded and smiled. "I'm glad to know you, Jonathan Moseley. I'll see ya in a couple days."

They shook hands again, and her smile was reciprocated as the two boys walked into the night. She watched them, shadows in the light of the moon, until they disappeared.

———————————

Ceely found the walk between her house and that of Father Brown's to be a pleasant one, despite the heat and dust. She enjoyed the quiet, the only sounds being her footsteps and the bugs moving through the grass to her left and right. Ceely looked out across the plain, watched the grass sway with the breeze, and thought it wasn't right for her to feel most safe here, now, alone.

She crossed the highway, and after trekking the west road for a bit, she arrived at the house of Father Brown. He sat, just as every Tuesday, watching her approach through the filthy window of the confession camper. Ceely entered without knocking and plopped down in her usual spot, an old swivel chair void of covering, padding, or the wheels it came with. She crossed one leg over the other and leaned back in her chair.

"Forgive me, Father, for I have sinned," she said robotically. "It has been one week since my last confession."

"Go on," replied Father Brown, his voice rising above and below the flowered bed sheet that separated them. A silence settled in, Father Brown leaning forward with elbow on knee, and he heard a long sigh. Ceely leaned forward, ripped back the sheet, and stared directly at him.

"Ceely, you—"

"Listen, I been thinkin' 'bout what we went over last week," she said with a wrinkled brow. Father Brown nodded in response. "I know you say that with Jesus, all the old laws and what-not are done for, but I think that's a mistake."

"How so?"

"Well, in the old times—"

"You mean the Old Testament times?" he asked, interrupting her.

"Yeah. Yeah, back then it was an eye for an eye," she sliced the air with both hands in opposite directions. "That's it."

"Uh-huh," replied Father Brown.

"Then with Jesus comin' 'round, you say all that changed, and now it's all about forgiveness. Sounds real convenient if ya ask me."

Over the past weeks, the priest had become completely enamored with this young lady. Each week he looked forward to her visit, as well as the intense debates, always followed by a lunch prepared at the hand of his wife. Ceely's honesty, her willingness to question, was refreshing to him. He narrowed his eyes and looked out the window to his right as he gathered his response.

"I don't know about convenient," he said, "but certainly easier. Which is, of course, the point."

"Whaddya mean?" she asked, crossing her arms in suspicion.

"I mean that God, in His mercy, is offering forgiveness for simply believing and performing the sacred rituals. Not hard. Easy."

"Convenient," replied Ceely. "I like the old way better. You do somethin' wrong, it gets done to you. Period. Is it time for lunch yet?"

She was the most honest person he had ever met. He looked down and shook his head, gave a slight laugh, and replied with a chuckle, "Yes. It's about time."

Old Mrs. Brown, as the town knew her, was in fact nearing the completion of an early lunch in the home she shared with the town priest. A casserole—creamy, warm, crunchy on top—was approaching the perfect cook time in her oven. The smell permeated the air and assaulted Ceely's nose the minute she stepped in.

"Mmm-mmm," she said loudly after stepping inside the door.

"Little C?" came a voice from the kitchen. Mrs. Brown was a tiny woman, five feet tall with helmet-shaped brown hair, eyes heavy with mascara, and an apron constantly attached to her waist. She was an interesting mate for Father Brown. He was well over six feet tall, thin and awkward, yet they came together like a puzzle—complete and natural.

"Smells good, Mrs. Brown," Ceely offered as she sat down at the large, spotless kitchen table. She watched the priest's wife remove the dish from the oven and sit it down gently on an old, worn towel.

"Just in time." The priest joined his guest at the table just as Mrs. Brown set two steaming plates before them.

"I suppose the two of you debated again this morning?" Mrs. Brown asked as she returned to the kitchen.

"Miss Ceely keeps me on my toes, that's for sure," her husband replied just before he shoveled a bite.

Ceely, without removing attention from her plate, gave a snort of laughter.

Father Brown smiled. "Though I believe she might just come for the food."

———————————

Ceely next saw Jonathan Moseley before she expected to and in a place she didn't predict: her front steps. After lunch at Father Brown's, she had come home and showered. She heard the doorbell ringing as soon as she stepped out and was shocked to see him standing politely on the other side of the door.

"Hello John," she said as she opened the clear glass door.

"Miss Ceely," he replied, a bit embarrassed. He cleared his throat. "I...uh...was in the area and thought I would make sure you were doin' okay."

"Very kind of you," she said with a grin. "Won't you come in?"

He accepted her invitation, and the two of them sat on opposite ends of the sofa in the living room. The house was silent, save the sound of breathing and a whirling ceiling fan overhead, and John thought it very nice.

"Do your parents know you are out and about today?" she asked, breaking the silence.

"Yeah. No. I don't know," he said with a shrug. "I told Mom, but she doesn't pay much attention when I talk."

"She just ignores you?" Ceely asked.

"Pretty much," he replied. "They're always sleepin' and stuff. Just lazy."

"Except when they get mad at you," Ceely said in a low tone.

He nodded, his eyes heavy, and stared out at nothing. "Yeah. 'Cept then."

Over the next hour, the two of them talked about more pleasant things. Ceely learned of his likes, his dislikes, the grandparents in Dallas, and various other things. He was very well spoken for a child so young. She found him charming.

"What about you?" he asked.

What about me?"

"Anything," he said.

Ceely stared at the carpet, her hand on her cheek, and thought about the question. What about her? She could tell him about the numbness she felt. She could discuss her enormous desire to escape this house, this road, this town. She had often wished to be a bird. She envied their freedom. They were strong and capable. The reach of one's dreams is relative to their current situation. She had read that somewhere.

She shrugged. "I don't know."

John turned his eyes slowly away from her. He seemed disappointed.

"Whatcha gonna do with all those pictures?" he asked, scratching a knee.

It was a question she had asked herself many times. No one had ever asked her until now, and she felt unprepared to answer, despite the hours of thought she had given to the subject. She sat forward and placed her elbows on her knees.

"Not sure yet, John boy. Somethin.'"

It made her think of her grandfather. He was a man she greatly loved and respected but had not seen in several months. Her mother and grandfather had fallen out, and because of that, her mother had forbidden the two to see each other. It was a painful separation, though Ceely endured it, as she had done everything else in her short life.

"Guess I better be goin,'" John Moseley said after a few moments.

"Thank you very much for the visit," she replied. He turned and gave a shy wave as he opened the door and was gone.

Two weeks later, Ceely Dawn was in good spirits. Her mother was the same as always, but her mother's husband had been out of town for three days and wasn't

Jeremy Mark Lane

due back for two more. It was a pleasure not having him around. She felt free, unafraid, and it was odd, but she thought she felt herself standing straighter as she walked. The day was closing in on ten o'clock, and she decided she wanted to read. She rummaged through the back corner of her closet until she found her favorite, a worn copy of short stories by Truman Capote. The front cover was ripped off and the back nearly so, but all of the stories remained intact. "His novels are good," she once told her English teacher, "but his stories are better."

Ceely read until midnight, the only light coming from a candle on her nightstand. After glancing at the clock, she set her book down, blew out the candle, and quietly left the room. The heat of the summer night surrounded her as soon as she stepped out the back door and onto the porch. As she had done so many times before, she followed the path down toward the pebblestone then, finding her spot, knelt down and gave the usual "Coo." The call was returned, and she walked in. The moon shone down on her friends. Todd, Little Dave, and Katie were all there. Everyone except little John Moseley.

"Where's John boy?" Ceely asked as the kids gathered around her.

Todd shrugged. "Not sure. I went by his house today. Knocked. No answer," he said. "Think he left town or something?" Ceely asked after a moment.

"Not sure," Little Dave replied.

"Hmmm," was her response.

Ceely was pleased to find all of the kids in good shape. Either through good timing or good luck, they had all managed to come through the last week unscathed. Crickets chirped across the field as they sat silently on the edge of the pebblestone.

"We won't be this way forever," Ceely said, breaking the silence.

"Whaddya mean?" Katie asked.

Ceely sighed. "I mean ... I mean we won't be young forever. We'll be adults one day. When you're an adult, no one hurts you unless you let 'em."

No one spoke.

"Promise me you won't let 'em," she said.

"Promise," they all responded within a second of one another.

Me too, Ceely thought to herself.

Jeremy Mark Lane

––––––––––––––––––

The humidity was well settled by the time Ceely left the house the next morning. Sweat was forming on her nose before she made it to the end of her driveway. It was hard to believe a person could be sweating at eight o'clock in the morning. She was headed to Father Brown's, and on her way planned to stop by little John Moseley's house. She felt for sure he was out of town, but she wanted to stop anyway.

As she walked, she looked up and saw a bird on the highline. It looked this way and that, prepared to fly at the smallest sign of disturbance. The bird was small, even frail, but it was free. She was envious. "Oh, to fly away," she said in a whisper. "This very minute. While I'm still myself and can be something to someone." She watched the bird, still walking, until her neck tired of looking up, and she returned her gaze to the white-hot road. Up ahead was the young boy's house.

It seemed that no one was home, but still she climbed the steps onto the porch. Several knocks, then a ring of the doorbell, and nothing. She felt sure they had gone, but still, she turned the doorknob. It was unlocked.

The door creaked as it opened then was silent. She stood motionless in the doorway. "Hello," she called to no answer. "Hello?" She knew she shouldn't, but her feet stepped inside. One step after another through the living room, down the hall, and to a cluster of bedroom doors. Two open, darkness inside, and a closed third. She reached and opened it much like she had the front door and let it creep open.

It was a child's room, no doubt, with athletes on the wall and dirty laundry on the floor. Her eyes scanned everything in her sight. Then she opened the door a bit more and gazed upon the boy lying in the bed. He slept soundly, though not peacefully. His face was bruised badly and his breathing was labored.

"John boy," she said under her breath.

Footsteps sounded outside on the porch, and Ceely's breath was lost. She looked to her left, spotted a closet door, opened it, and slipped inside without a sound. She listened, holding her breath as the footsteps grew louder. They came to a stop in the doorway of Jonathan's bedroom.

The crack of the closet door let in enough light that once her eyes adjusted she could see the closet floor. Next to her feet sat a red Swiss army knife. Her grandfather had given her one several years back; it rested in her dresser drawer.

"You leave that door open?" asked a loud, gravelly voice.

Ceely reached down quickly and picked up the knife.

"Hey!" the voice grew louder. Ceely found the largest blade and took it from its position. The light through the door shone on the silver.

"Hey!" She heard the bed move and the boy moan.

In one quick motion she threw open the door, lunged toward her target, and plunged the knife into his neck once, then twice more. The lumbering man crumpled to the floor, and there lay Jonathan Moseley. His eyes were only partly open. Ceely was trembling and felt the warmth of blood on her hand. The young boy looked at her in a strange way. It was not a look of fear, nor terror, but a look of relief through narrow, tired eyes. Ceely stood still, and for a moment it seemed that she drifted out of herself and was hovering above all of them; she was struck with her own calmness. Her hands did not shake and her breathing was only slightly accelerated. She dropped the knife and wiped her hands down the front of her shirt. It left streaks of blood.

"John boy," she said. "John boy, I want you to call 911 as soon as I leave. Tell 'em exactly what happened. You understand?"

He was sitting up in bed now, still groggy but alert. He nodded. "Tell 'em everything," she said and left the house.

From that moment on, everything played out like a dream for Ceely Dawn. She knew it was real, but her mind, her vision, her movements felt different. She walked to Katie's house and knocked on the window.

"Ceely, you coulda come to the door," Katie said to her then looked at her blood-stained shirt with wide, questioning eyes.

"Give me the pictures," Ceely replied.

She did so, and Ceely escaped into the barren field to the north. She found a gully to lie down in, and soon she heard the sound of an ambulance siren piercing the quiet town she had spent her whole life in. Nothing would be the same. Not ever again.

Long after nightfall, she walked the distance to her home. As she expected, there were several police cars in the drive, all with red lights illuminating the desolate landscape. She stepped quietly up to the front porch, opened the door, and stepped in. She calmly scanned the room and met the eyes of Father Brown, seemingly on the verge of tears; her mother, eyes bloodshot and wet; and her grandfather, who stood and waited for her next move. Several other policemen filled the small living room to capacity.

Ceely Dawn unzipped the bag as she took slow, deliberate steps toward her grandfather, and once within an arm's length of him, she dropped the wad of photos on the ground.

"They're just children," she said. "Just kids." She then turned to Father Brown, now crying at the sight of such evil, and said, "Eye for an eye."

Later, in the passenger seat of her grandfather's squad car, Ceely watched the moon as it beamed down upon the earth. The car paused at the end of the dirt road she had walked so many times, and Ceely spotted five birds resting on a high line just before they pulled onto the highway. *What a strange sight at this hour*, she thought. Four of the birds took flight simultaneously while the fifth held its ground. Then, just as the outline of the moon shifted to a new location, she saw the last bird take to the air. It was a freedom to be envied.

Shape

Snowfall in the Deep South is at once a source of delirious joy and terrible aggravation. The joy is supplied by the children, and it comes in its most concentrated form, a reminder to the world that it is all right to wish a given day would never end. They run shrieking out of the house, unaware that the cancelling of school is only the beginning of the fantastic happenings of life, and quickly run back in to search for a jacket and gloves.

People in the warmer parts of America are largely unprepared for such drastic weather, so the children begin displaying an admirable ingenuity. Sleds and snowboards are constructed from plywood, flattened cardboard boxes, and for the very young, plastic container lids. Some are pushed up and down the street by a sibling or friend, while others are pulled along thanks to an old rope and the neighbor's riding lawn-mower, and they all migrate to the side of the road in the event of a passing car.

It is these passersby who, as if required to balance out the universe, carry with them the aforementioned aggravation. It is not intentional; it simply happens that the adult life carries on despite the weather, and as in the case of Tommy West, it sometimes grows more troublesome. He'd just finished pouring his son's cereal when the call came from his brother.

"Guess the weather turned on us," his brother said.

"Yep. Five or six inches, I'd guess," Tommy replied.

"Wish I could get there to see it. I'm stuck in Jacksonville. Not sure when I'll get a flight out."

"Need me to check on Mary and the kids?" Tommy asked. His brother lived near downtown; it was only a few minutes away.

"Nah, I just talked to them. They're fine. Kids probably have frostbite by now." Tommy watched as his three-year-old son operated the spoon. A trail of milk rolled down his chin.

"I do need a favor, though," his brother continued. "The nursing home called me this morning, said it could be any time now."

"Isn't that always what they say?" Tommy said sarcastically.

"I know," his brother replied. "Help me out?"

Tommy was not one to deny his brother, so he agreed, but with resentment. The care of his mother in her declining years had always been the worry of his older brother, and it was an arrangement that Tommy preferred.

Their parents had been married for seventeen years. During their time together, they had two children, though only one was raised to adulthood with both parents in the home. They separated as Tommy was entering his freshman year of high school, a time in life already replete with its own barely manageable serving of angst. The problems at home had been an unwelcomed addition, and he blamed them, perhaps without realizing it, for his own missteps, namely the inability to maintain a relationship for any respectable amount of time.

The separation of Tommy and the mother of his son had been the most recent and by far the most damaging of his failed attempts at love. She was perfect for him in every conceivable way, yet he'd figured out a way of eventually tearing it all down, as if quickening the inevitable in the interest of self-preservation. What love ever really lasted?

It was a good thing that disappointment did not come easy at three years old. While all of the children in the city were laughing and playing in the snow, Tommy told his son he would have to spend some time at the house of Mrs. Cooley, the next-door neighbor, and he responded only with "Okay." Tommy decided the key to happiness was to never know what you were missing, and for a moment, he envied his son for that very reason.

Mrs. Cooley was approaching eighty years old but exhibited the energy and resourcefulness of someone half her age. She was widowed and spent most of her time cooking. This left Tommy with a supply of so many casseroles that when his own refrigerator was filled to capacity, he would be forced to find others to pass the dishes on to. Mrs. Cooley had lived so long that the sheer volume of life experience she had accumulated gave her the ability to discern the state of Tommy's life simply by the way he knocked on the door. She gave him a sympathetic nod as he walked his son into her house. He kissed the boy, told him he'd be back as soon as possible, and left for the nursing home.

It was roughly ten miles from Tommy's house to the nursing home, and he avoided the interstate in favor of the neighborhood streets blanketed in white. In almost predictable intervals there would be a group of children playing, running, laughing. He would slow as they huddled at the curb, smiling as he passed, then scatter back into the streets like ants once he was gone. As he drove, he contemplated the tendency of life to remove the childhood smile and replace it with something far less enjoyable, perhaps worry, exhaustion, or both.

Completely forgetting that the smell of a nursing home made him queasy, Tommy had not prepared himself, and his stomach knotted when he walked in the front door. The woman at the front desk had been watching him, now standing just inside the front entrance, and asked him, "Are you all right, sir?"

"Yes, yes," he said. "I'm here to see Nadine West."

"Oh, okay," she replied, her expression slightly changed. "Just one second." She vanished down a hallway and a few seconds later returned with a man in a white coat following behind her. He held his hand out to Tommy as he approached.

"Tommy, I'm Dr. Clark. Your brother told me you were coming." Tommy nodded as they shook hands. "I'm afraid the pneumonia's back," he said. "We knew it would be at some point."

"Right," Tommy said, while something like surprise, or maybe guilt, spread over him. He knew nothing of the pneumonia.

"At this point, I've given instructions to keep her comfortable in her room, as the family requested last time," the doctor said.

"Okay, right," was all Tommy could say. He was giving his best impression of someone privy to the situation, though he clearly was not.

The doctor watched him for a moment, waiting for questions, then spoke again. "I've got to get back to the hospital. The staff here has my pager number if you need anything at all."

They said good-bye, and the girl at the front led Tommy down a long hallway past a series of open rooms. Some were silent, while others emitted the faint sounds of a television at low volume. She stopped at the last door on the right, told him to see her for anything he needed, and went back the way they'd come.

He stepped in slowly, unsure of what to expect, and found her asleep. A few wires ran to and from her frail body, and the color of her skin did not match the memory of the last time he'd seen her. Her mouth was slightly open, as if on the verge of speech. He was struck by her hair; it was thin and appeared brittle. She had always kept a thick, healthy head of hair.

He turned away his eyes for fear that she would awaken and ask him questions he did not want to answer. *You're angry with me, aren't you?* He didn't want to talk about it. *Stop trying to get everyone to talk about things.* He was angry for a moment—angry at the inquisition—before realizing that she hadn't spoken a word. There was only the steady, shallow sound of labored breathing.

Tommy walked over to the window and slid the curtain back just enough to give a narrow view of the outside snow. He wanted assurance that places existed beyond the room he was in. Sitting down in a corner chair, he propped his head against the wall and did his best to get lost in the silence.

It had been several minutes, or maybe hours—he didn't know—when the sound of footsteps began to echo down the hallway outside. They grew closer and closer until stopping in the doorway of his mother's room. He turned slowly, expecting a nurse, and instead found an elderly man with a sun-spotted face, narrow spectacles, and a thin ring of hair reaching from temple to temple. He wore khaki slacks and a horribly mismatched flannel shirt.

"You may have the wrong room, sir," Tommy whispered. "This is Nadine West."

The man pursed his lips, glanced at Tommy, and stepped into the room. He walked straight over to the bed. Tommy watched in confusion as he softly gripped her hand with his own and caressed it gently with the other. It was the touch of something more than friendship, and Tommy felt uncomfortable. After a moment, the man walked over to the empty chair next to Tommy and sat down.

"I've got the right room," he said quietly.

"Forgive me, I don't think we've met," Tommy replied.

"Frank," the man said, and they shook hands.

"You're a friend of my mother's, I take it?"

"Was. Many years ago, I was," he replied. "Which son are you?"

"Tommy. The youngest."

The man nodded and let out a long exhale as he relaxed in his chair. They sat in silence for several minutes. Tommy was unsure of what to say, while the expression on the elderly man's face showed he was content with saying nothing. Finally, he spoke.

"It's my fault, you know," he said.

"What? The pneumonia?" Tommy replied.

"Oh, no. That's the fault of time. The fault of the body."

"Then what do you mean?"

"Her life. Her life's my fault. At least partly," he said.

"I guess I don't understand what you—"

"You're angry with her," said the old man. "As you should be."

He was right, of course. Of his two parents, Tommy was far more resentful toward his mother. She'd been the one who left, and she'd fallen in love with her sudden freedom and lack of responsibility.

93

As is always the case, that approach to life magnetizes one to people of a similar ilk, and all of them view life in permanently temporary manner. What is right today may be wrong tomorrow, and after enough time passes, they inevitably find themselves alone. This had happened to Tommy's mother, and after so many years, the guilt she carried, especially in regard to her youngest son, weighed so heavily that she deemed it pointless to attempt a repair.

"Tell me, how do you know my mother?" Tommy asked.

"We were in love once. When we were very young, we were in love," he replied.

Tommy raised his eyebrows in surprise.

"You're shocked that we were in love or that we were once young?" he asked with a slight grin. "Your mother was wonderful," he said, turning his eyes back to the hospital bed. "What we had, it was that thing you find once, then you spend the rest of your life measuring with it."

Tommy had no idea what to say or what to think.

"We would've married for sure. Would've spent a wonderful life together, if it weren't for that night."

Tommy was not interested in hearing more but felt certain that the man would continue anyway.

"That night?" he asked.

"The ol' Parker place. We all used to go out there. Go out in the pasture and just talk, listen to music, drink beer. Just have fun," he said.

"I'm gonna get some coffee," Tommy said. "Want some?"

"I think you should hear this," the man replied.

Tommy sat back in his chair.

"That night some girl, somebody's cousin or somethin,' she kept on flirting with me. You know how it is. I didn't exactly shut it down. Your mother was pretty jealous."

Tommy was wishing he could leave, that his brother hadn't gotten stuck in Jacksonville, that he had never asked him to come here.

"She got real mad. We'd been drinking. Finally, I got fed up and I ... I wasn't even thinking. I'm not a man who raises his hand to a woman." The old man shook his head in remorse.

Tommy looked at his mother.

"She left, and I didn't go after her. I should have gone after her. Let me tell you, son, it's a terrible thing to live a lifetime regretting something that happened in one minute. It's a terrible thing."

He turned, and Tommy saw his eyes swelling with tears. "It's those minutes that make your shape."

"Your shape?" Tommy asked.

"Yes, your shape. You see, a person's shape doesn't stay the same. It's molded over time. It's life. It's your shape."

"Your shape," Tommy said with a sigh.

The old man nodded. "Takes a hell of a lot of work to fix what you've broken. Most don't want to give the effort. Figure it's too late. That includes me, and I was wrong for it. Doing my best now to make it right. While I'm still myself and can make amends."

With that, the old man stood and walked back toward the bed. He touched her hand lightly and made for the doorway. "Take care, Tommy," he said and was gone.

Tommy left the hospital in late afternoon. The staff promised to call if things went bad before morning, and he made his way back through the neighborhoods where the children still played in the snow-covered streets. His son was stacking blocks in the living room floor when he arrived back at Mrs.

Cooley's house. He was surprised to find Jessica, the boy's mother, seated cross-legged on the floor next to him.

"I just came by to see him real quick," she said.

"Sure. Good," Tommy replied.

"I made a lasagna," said Mrs. Cooley from the kitchen. She walked over and handed him a covered glass dish. "Figured you'd had a long day."

"Yes ma'am, thank you," Tommy said. He watched as Jessica kissed their son good-bye, and the three of them stepped into the yard together. "Headed out somewhere?" Tommy asked.

"Just home," she replied.

"I doubt we can eat all this," he said, raising the dish. "You're welcome to join us."

She looked at him for a moment. "Um, okay," she said.

Later, they sat at the dinner table together. It was the picture of what was once a small family now existing as two separate pieces as the warmth of the food made them forget about the cold.

"Let's get a full stomach," Tommy said to his son. "I thought we'd make a sled this evenin.' Maybe your mom could help us."

The boy's eyes lit up as he smiled. It was the look of one who wished the day would go on forever, and Tommy, as much as any adult can, found himself wishing the same.

Souls in the Wind

James Briscoe stood looking out the window of his study. He often came upstairs in the midmorning and poured himself two fingers of whiskey. It wasn't an honorable practice to be drinking this early in the day—he knew that—yet he found it relaxing. It was his time to think.

On this particular morning he watched as Polly Ann, the daughter of Smoke Jackson, his most reliable and highest-paid farmhand, walked out of the barn, where his son was tinkering with an old wagon. Normally he wouldn't have given it a second thought, except that James had witnessed several suspicious things of late and was watching with a careful eye.

A man has a way of knowing when something is different within his own universe, and the shy conversations, quick smiles, and fleeting glances between his son and the young girl had perked his attention. He felt no need to forbid his son to speak with Polly, or anyone else for that matter. It was the girl's beauty that worried him, and her color, which caused a different kind of apprehension.

Something caught his eye as he took a sip from the glass. Along the eastern edge of the cornfield ran a tree line, with a solitary tree one hundred yards to the west. Under the tree were two horses, both riders dismounted, and a third man, who looked to be on his knees. Briscoe set his whiskey on the window ledge and hurried down the stairs, out the door, and into the barn. He pulled his horse from the first pen and mounted with no saddle.

"Where you goin,' Pop?" his son asked as he rode by, his horse agitated at the quick mount. Briscoe knew it wasn't any of his hands; he could recognize his men from five hundred yards just by the way they stood. He rode at a gallop down into the field and followed the eastern tree line toward the men and horses. A black man, no doubt the one on his knees before, was now standing with his hands tied behind his back. Briscoe approached and spotted the white of a noose around his neck. "Mornin,' Mr. Briscoe," said one of the other men. He knew the voice right away. It was Hank Aldridge, the overzealous young sheriff of Wichita Falls.

Aldridge was a skinny pencil of a man who'd once chased someone from Wichita Falls to Denton for stealing two tomatoes from a widow's garden. The sheriff tracked him to a saloon there, bound and gagged the man, and dragged him terrified to the local jail. Upon hearing the man's infraction, the local lawman agreed to jail the vegetable thief but informed Hank that he would be incarcerated as well for disturbing a local business over such a small matter. The young sheriff left humiliated, and the story traveled back to Wichita Falls quicker than his worn-out horse. He was a laughing stock among most in his town, and James Briscoe was among those with little respect for the man.

"What the hell's goin' on here, Hank?" Briscoe asked as he hopped down from his horse.

"Now, Mr. Briscoe, I asked you before to call me 'Sheriff,'" Aldridge replied, looking up from under the brim of his hat.

"All right, Sheriff, what the hell's goin' on here and what are you doin' on my land?"

Aldridge spit and wiped his mouth with the back of his shirtsleeve. "This boy was caught with a white woman. Lady said he come on strong. She couldn't fend him off."

"And I guess you believe that too, don't you?" Briscoe said with a smirk.

"It's grounds for a lynchin,' and you know it, James," the sheriff replied.

"Yeah, I know that. Another thing I know is that—" They were suddenly interrupted by an unnatural sound. Briscoe turned to find the black man dangling from the noose, the rope flung over the tree and tight around the deputy's saddle horn. The deputy held his horse steady while the black man gagged, twitched, then hung lifelessly. Briscoe watched the man die then looked down at the ground and tightened the hat on his head. He turned to the sheriff. Briscoe was a large man, well over six foot, with broad shoulders and a muscular frame. He walked slowly, until his nose nearly touched the sheriff's.

"Have your man turn loose of that rope," he said sternly. Aldridge watched him through squinted eyes. He gave his deputy a nod, and the black man crumpled to the ground.

"Now get off my land, and if I ever catch you on my property again, I'll shoot ya."

"Doubt you'd shoot a lawman," replied Aldridge.

"That's true. You ain't one."

The sheriff turned slowly, walked to his horse, and mounted. He rode off in silence with his deputy following behind. Briscoe watched them until they were out of sight then mounted his horse and rode toward home without looking at the body. He looked up to find Jordy several paces away from the barn. He was standing in between two rows of corn and must have witnessed the whole episode. Standing a hundred feet behind him, next to the barn, was Smoke Jackson. James was aggravated that either had seen the hanging. He rode up to Jordy and stopped his horse.

"What are you gonna do, Pop?" the boy asked.

"Dig that man a grave," Briscoe replied, looking behind him.

"You want me to help?"

"No, son, I don't,"

Briscoe tied his horse and found Smoke had already brought two shovels.

"Take the rest of the day off, Smoke," he said.

"Let me help ya dig, Mr. Briscoe," Smoke replied.

"No need. Spend the day with your family," he said in a tone that offered no option for rebuttal. Smoke gave a slight nod and walked away. James once again mounted his horse, more gently this time, and allowed the animal to turn a full circle. He watched as Smoke put an arm around his wife and guided her into their small house, then looked over to find Jordy and Polly Ann in an awkward conversation, both looking at the ground rather than each other. He turned his horse and trotted off, intent on providing the stranger in his field a proper grave.

The happenings of the night are most often dependent upon the previous day, and because of this, some nights are not made for sleeping. James Briscoe was a firm believer in rest because he was a firm believer in work, so sitting in the dark of his study well after nightfall caused him to feel something like guilt.

He was unsure exactly what was unsettling him. The stranger was not the first man who had died before his eyes, though Briscoe knew in his heart that the hanging had been needless; Aldridge was far too incompetent to serve anything resembling justice. His mind kept drifting back to Jordy and the young girl, the sum of everything he had seen over the previous weeks, and their melancholy conversation after the terrible event. He wondered what his son had said to her in such a moment, if he had spoken as a boy or a man.

As if on cue, Briscoe caught sight of a white cotton dress swaying in the night breeze, moving away from the Jackson house and into the field. A strong moon allowed him to watch as she made her way into the cornfield, alone and at a quick pace, before disappearing into the shadows of the night. He did not move from his seat, as he did not desire to desecrate what he suspected might be happening, so he did not witness as the young girl spoke whispers of sorrow to the fresh, raised dirt, and as she placed a flower at the head of the grave under the solitary tree. These things he did not witness, though he knew them just the same.

Despite the late night, Briscoe woke just after sunup, dressed, and walked outside. He enjoyed being the first one out, though he rarely did any work this early. He mostly enjoyed the quiet—the sound of the wind shuffling the grass in the field and the rustling of the trees. He stood in the open air and took in the sounds around him. He thought about the day's work. It was a good feeling to know those he loved were still asleep.

The slam of a screen door shattered the quiet morning, and he turned to see Smoke crossing the yard with a hurried walk. As he drew near, Briscoe noticed a ghastly look on his face. "Mornin' Smoke," he said loudly.

"Mistuh Briscoe," replied Smoke. "Mistuh Briscoe."

"What's wrong?"

"It's Polly," he said with a faltering voice. "She's gone."

"Gone? Gone where?"

"See fuh yourself, suh," Smoke replied, and offered a folded letter.

His heart nearly stopped as he read the words Polly had written. He stared at the paper long after he had finished reading it, trying to formulate a response, trying to absorb the situation. He had little concern about Jordy's ability to make it on his own. He was a strong, intelligent boy. It was different for Smoke. Having an attractive young black girl out on the plains was another matter.

He glanced over to Jordy's window.

"Guess you didn't check his room this mornin,' Mistuh Briscoe," Smoke said.

"Nah. Rarely do. Figure I'll let him sleep while he can."

The screen door sounded again, and Briscoe looked over to see Smoke's wife on the porch, her hand covering her mouth to stifle the sobs.

"Go calm your wife. I'll go and see if the boy left a letter. Then we'll talk about what we're gonna do."

He put a hand on Smoke's shoulder and made for the house.

He opened the door quietly, hoping not to encounter his wife, and heard no movement. A few quick steps took him to Jordy's door, which he opened. He found an empty bed. Though he had expected it, the sight of his son's neatly folded sheets had a strange effect on him. On the pillow was an unfolded letter with fifty dollars resting on top.

> Pop,
> I took a little food and two horses. Here is fifty dollars. I hope you are not angry. I just love her. Kiss Momma for me, and tell her not to worry.
>
> Jordy

It was impossible for him to be angry. James was a reasonable and levelheaded man, yet he had done some stupid things in his life, and nearly every one of them because of a girl. Jordy had the spirit for adventure; it was a trait shared by his father.

The corner of a few papers sticking out of the nightstand caught Briscoe's attention. He opened the drawer and found a few scribblings, some numbers, and a map of Texas. A route south was penciled here and there, and a note at the bottom read: *Galveston, 600 miles*.

James leaned back and sighed loudly.

Half an hour later he sat in the family room, listening patiently while his wife and Mrs. Jackson took turns sobbing and railing against the foolishness of their children. His wife's reaction was just what he'd expected—she had always been a dramatic woman— but he was surprised at Mrs. Jackson. He had known her for years, and though they rarely conversed, she always appeared stern, though polite, and insistent on proper behavior. James wondered at the power of a child to create such heartache. It was a power held by children alone.

Briscoe's patience thinned, and he interrupted his wife.

"All right," he said and sat forward with his elbows on his knees. "We all agree what they did was foolish, and we wish they hadn't, but they did." Both women were fidgeting with their tissues and sniffling.

"Now, as I see it, we probably oughta go find 'em. If it was just my boy, I wouldn't worry so much, but young Polly …"

The mention of Polly's name wrenched Mrs. Jackson, and she fought back tears. Smoke consoled her with a hand on the knee.

"Mistuh Briscoe," Smoke said. "I'm all fuh goin' after 'em, but they could be off in any direction now."

Briscoe nodded and scratched his neck. "I got a pretty good idea where they might be headed," he replied. "Believe they may be tryin' for Galveston."

His wife gasped. "Galveston? Oh, Lord, what for?"

"All that talk my nephew gave him, I'm sure." Smoke gave him a confused look. "Word is Galveston's, um, progressive," Briscoe said. Smoke shuffled in his seat.

"How do ya mean, suh?"

"Well," he replied and turned both palms upward. "It's easier for black folks. Better than most places. That's what they say."

Smoke shook his head in disbelief. "I don't undastand," he said. "Polly was always treated just fine right here on this farm."

"I appreciate your sayin' that. Fact is, though, this is a little farm compared to a big ol' world. 'Spect they was impatient to see a bit of it." Silence set in, and Briscoe sat back in his chair.

"When do we leave, Mistuh Briscoe?" Smoke asked after a moment.

"'Round sundown. Horses will travel better out of the sunlight."

"Won't they just get farther away?" asked his wife.

"They're pullin' a wagon. We'll catch 'em quick enough," he replied and rose from his chair. "Y'all sit as long as you like," he said then made for the stairs. He needed a drink.

James spent the afternoon gathering the things he would need for the trip. He planned to travel light, making it easier on his horse, and to carry enough cash to purchase what he might otherwise need. He gave Smoke his pick of a horse, along with his own suggestion, and instructions to pack light as he had done.

After consoling his wife once more and promising a swift return, Briscoe led his horse out into the evening sun. The farmhands would on any other day have been gone to do whatever it was they did at night, but they sensed something strange and stood around making small talk not far from Smoke's porch. Briscoe was aware of them watching him; he gave a motion for them to come over. Smoke stood with his horse on one side and his wife on the other, just behind the rest of the boys.

"Me and Smoke are gonna be gone for a few days," he said loudly. "While we're gone, Mrs. Jackson will be in charge." Briscoe caught a look of surprise on some faces.

"She's got authority to fire you, though I don't anticipate her needin' to. Just do what you do when we're here." He nodded, and the group dispersed. Smoke and his wife approached slowly.

"You 'bout ready?" Briscoe asked.

Smoke nodded. "Yes, suh."

"Mrs. Jackson, if you need anything bought, just let my wife know."

"I'll take care a' things, Mistuh Briscoe," she said. The distraught woman from inside the house had disappeared, and Briscoe recognized her again. "You find my Polly, Mistuh Briscoe. While I'm still myself and can stand up straight."

"Yes'm. I will," he replied, and mounted his horse. He trotted ahead to give them time to say good-bye.

While I'm Still Myself

Briscoe couldn't remember the last time he had ridden off into the brush. He began to realize just how comfortable life had become. The sound of Smoke's horse came from behind, and he fought back a smile. People were worried, and with good reason, but Briscoe couldn't help but feel glad to be leaving.

———————————

The two men made good time through the evening and into the night. A full moon sparkled on the sides of the sweating horses, yet Briscoe was adamant that they stop only long enough to give the animals water and a short rest. He began to feel that a full moon on a warm night was just what he had needed—he was almost jolly but did not let on as much to Smoke—as he conjured up memories of his youth, before fatigue existed for him, riding and hunting and answering to no one.

"What you suppose drives a child to run off, Mistuh Briscoe?" Smoke asked.

"Ah, hell," he replied. "Lotsa things. Love. Hate. Fear. You name it."

"Never thought I'd be chasin' young Polly, though. Always been a good child."

"Still is," Briscoe said. "Both are. Can't hold a little romance against 'em. Had my share, and I'm sure you did too."

Smoke gave a quiet laugh and shook his head. "Yessuh. That's true enough."

Later, the morning hour began to paint a gray light across the countryside, and the cool breeze of the darkness transformed to the muggy still of a July day. The tip of the morning sun reached the horizon, illuminating a small camp about a mile ahead. Briscoe spotted the wagon through his field glasses and nudged his horse.

"There they are. Let's go," he said in Smoke's direction.

Both horses were spent. It occurred to him that they would need a day's rest before making the trip home. His body tensed as he closed the distance to the camp and caught sight of an extra horse and a third person.

Briscoe knew immediately who it was, and his horse was at a full gallop when he dismounted. Jordy was sitting on the ground with his hands tied behind his back. Polly, her cheeks wet with tears, was at the back of the wagon, and Hank Aldridge stood near the morning fire.

"Aldridge," Briscoe said through clenched teeth, his eyes wild with fury. He was two strides away when the sheriff pulled his gun.

"Settle down, now, Mr. Briscoe."

Briscoe hesitated then took another step. "What the hell do you think you're doing?" he said.

"Seems your boy's in some trouble," Aldridge replied. "Kidnappin' this young girl here. Not good at all." He shook his head dramatically.

"Nobody's been kidnapped. They left together by choice."

"Hmm. Doubt that. Either way, he'll be goin' back with me," Aldridge replied.

"Damned if he will."

Movement from the side caused both Briscoe and Aldridge to turn their heads. Polly walked quietly to Jordy, fell to her knees, and wrapped her arms gently around his neck. Her tears dampened the collar of his shirt.

"Hey! Get away from that boy," Aldridge yelled, his gun now pointed in their direction. "Hey!" he yelled again and began walking toward them.

An explosion sent Briscoe stumbling backward, his vision blurred and ears ringing. He looked down at himself, feeling and searching for the wound, but found none. His vision focused, and he saw Smoke standing with a rifle, the smoke still fluttering out of the barrel, and Hank Aldridge's body crumpled on the ground. Blood poured from a hole in his neck.

Smoke looked over with a trembling face. It was at that moment that Briscoe finally understood the man he had known for so many years. The same unquenchable fire burned within Smoke Jackson as burns within every man, the unwillingness to relinquish those things ordained by God: freedom, the ability to protect those you love, equality in justice, happiness, peace. He felt, as they all did, retribution for the man buried under the tree.

Briscoe gathered himself, gave a slight nod, and walked over to untie his son.

Moments later, the two men stood with their children in silence, each of them exchanging looks of understanding. The events of the morning would belong to their memories alone.

Briscoe walked slowly over to a large, white rock with a pointed edge and picked it up with both hands.

"Where ya goin,' Pop?" Jordy asked.

"Dig that man a grave," Briscoe replied as a quick, cool breeze brought the smell of an oncoming rain.

Round Bale

When he turned fourteen, Dillon Steele arranged to spend an entire summer with his grandfather, Stanley Weedle. Mr. Weedle had done many things during his lifetime, often doing them simultaneously and always doing them well. At an early age, he'd built and raced hopped-up muscle cars and might have made something of it save a marriage at sixteen years old, a daughter shortly after, and another shortly after that. Later, he went into business, made himself a successful enterprise, sold it, and secured for himself a lifetime of income.

What he loved most, however, was the land. He harbored a deep love of the scraggly ground, poor grass, and skinny trees of the flat Texas countryside, and at the age of forty-three was able to purchase eighty-one acres of the best the great state had to offer. At the east end were acres of open field cultivated for various crops; in the center, a perfect nook covered in trees—the site of the Weedle home—and in the west, a jigsaw of cattle pens and a large, fully equipped dairy barn.

Such a barbaric profession as the dairy business did not exactly suit the finer tastes of Mr. Weedle. Those who knew him would scratch their heads and attempt to reconcile the man's preference for expensive food, wine, and furniture with the brutal and often unrewarding nature of working cattle, yet Stanley's uncles and father and grandfather had all made a living from cattle, and Dillon sensed it as an affront to his grandfather's manhood that one would suggest that he 'didn't have it in him' to do the same as they had done. So, upon purchasing the eighty-one acres, he stocked it with black and white cows, milk tanks, a family of hired hands, and went into the dairy business.

Dillon found the entire production to be magical. He would watch from the top of a pipe fence as the men walked along and beside the cattle, waving their arms and hollering words that were not words, some incredible language that only the men and cattle knew, and the cattle, who somehow knew to approach the barn entrance in a single file line. His longtime wish was to be old enough and big enough to play a part in the production, so it was to his dismay to find that the brunt of the work was now done by hydraulic machines and beeping digital controls while the men stood around and spit, the brown tobacco juice flowing to the large drain hole in the middle of the concrete floor.

His grandfather's primary assistant was a man named Cotton. If it was his given name, Dillon could not be sure, but in eavesdropping his grandparents' conversations, he'd learned that Cotton had somehow managed to marry his first cousin. The couple produced three children—two boys and a girl—all of varying levels of retardation.

"Milk's flowin' just fine, Mistuh Weedle," Cotton said late in the summer of '89.

"Yep," Stanley responded.

Dillon's eyes bounced back and forth between the two men, unwilling to miss a single word. It was late into the night and words were difficult to come by, so Dillon, fighting fatigue and boredom, made his way out of the barn and into the night air.

No one who visited the Weedle place ever saw Cotton's children during the daylight hours. They emerged from their dilapidated single-wide trailer house only two times per day—sunup and sundown—at which points the three of them would climb to the top of a single round bale of hay in the middle of a clearing between the house and the barn and watch in silence as the day began, then later as it came to an end.

As he stepped out of the barn, Dillon was surprised to see them out well after nightfall, loud and animated in the light of a full moon. He watched Tim, the younger son, pull himself off of the ground and stumble wildly, yelling incoherently, and Daisy, the obese younger sister, screaming and shoving violently against Ray, the oldest. Tim, now somewhat stable on his feet, darted into a frantic, clumsy run toward his older brother, and once within a few feet, leaped into a flailing tackle that took all three of them to the ground. Daisy let out with the piercing, unintelligible shriek of a wounded animal. Dillon strode back toward the barn door and stepped inside.

"Pops, I think you should come out here."

"What is it?"

"Not real sure, but I think you should come."

Stanley stepped out of the barn and listened as Dillon explained what he had seen. He knew his grandfather to stay out of other people's personal affairs, except for what happened on his own property.

"Go find out what happened," his grandfather said.

Dillon walked carefully toward the three of them, now all standing at distant corners of the clearing. He felt completely the responsibility to do what his grandfather had asked.

"Guys," he yelled. "Guys, come 'ere." They took slow steps in his direction.

Tim arrived first. He took his breaths in the manner of a horse, short and blunt; his hair was filthy with grass; and a mixture of blood and snot flowed out of his nose and rested on his upper lip. Dillon feared that the boy's brains were leaking out of his head. He stared at the ground. Dillon considered that his clothes could not be more mis-sized, as if the original owner was built as Tim's exact opposite in every extremity.

Daisy then stood with them. She was hideously ugly—it pained Dillon's stomach to look at her—with a man's mustache and cheeks covered with acne. Ray stood in the distance, his arms crossed in contempt.

"Guys, what's goin' on?" What happened?" Dillon asked. There was no response. "Guys?"

"Nothin,'" Tim grunted.

"Somethin' happened. I just saw you tryin' to kill each other." Again, no response.

Dillon walked back to his grandfather in defeat. "They won't talk," he said.

"Tim's the one got hit?" his grandfather asked.

"Yeah, I think so."

"Call him over and find out what happened."

Dillon was now regretting that he had any part in the situation. He waved Tim over.

"Did your brother hit you?"

The boy shrugged.

"I know you got hit. Your nose is bleedin.' Did Ray do it?"

The boy shrugged.

"C'mon, Tim. We're pals, right?"

The boy raised an eye to him.

"'Member that time I aired up that old soccer ball for ya?"

The boy nodded.

"All right, now, did your brother hit you?"

The boy nodded.

"What for?"

The boy shrugged.

"Tim, I'm upset over this. I wanna know why someone would hit my pal."

The boy sighed.

"Did ya get mad at each other?"

The boy nodded.

"'Bout what?"

"Daisy." The *s* in his sister's name came through his front teeth.

"What about her?"

The boy shrugged.

"Tim, c'mon."

The boy raised an eye to him.

"What about Daisy got y'all mad at each other?"

"Ray always sleep in Daisy room. Never Tim."

"Ray sleeps in Daisy's room?"

The boy nodded.

"And you never get to."

The boy nodded.

"Told Ray I's gonna tell on 'im."

"You told Ray you were gonna tell on him?"

The boy nodded.

"So he hit you."

The boy nodded.

"Tim, buddy. What's so great about sleepin' in Daisy's room anyway?"

The boy was silent.

Dillon approached his grandfather, who was standing impatiently at the corner of the barn, reported the conversation, and watched as Stanley's brow wrinkled deeper with each sentence.

"All right, go to the truck. We'll head home in just a second," his grandfather said.

Dillon watched his grandfather carefully approach Tim, give him a rag to clean his face, and pat him awkwardly on the shoulder. Stanley then called Cotton in a harsh tone. Dillon was just within earshot.

"By gawd, Misteh Weedle, don't know what I'm gonna do with those kids. Always fightin' lately. Help me, Mistuh Weedle, while I'm still myself, 'fore I lose my mind," Cotton pleaded.

"Shut up, Cotton," Stanley barked. "You're a good hand. Do good work here. What happens within your four walls is your business, but I'm very displeased with what I heard tonight. Fix it, or I will." Cotton nodded and stared at the ground.

Dillon's parents came early the next morning to pick him up. After breakfast and good-bye, they loaded into the car, and Dillon felt a familiar sadness at leaving the majestic eighty-one acres. Riding upon the white gravel road, he looked out his window into the gray early light and saw the shape of three children perched atop a single round bale, their faces turned to the horizon in search of the morning sun. It was the one thing they knew.

Made in the USA
Monee, IL
16 January 2022